For Niki, Eszter, The Mamas, and everyone
brave enough to say hello and goodbye

DIAL BOOKS FOR YOUNG READERS
An imprint of Penguin Random House LLC, New York

Copyright © 2019 by Cori Doerrfeld

Visit us online at penguinrandomhouse.com

Printed in China
ISBN 9780525554233

10 9 8 7 6 5 4 3 2 1

Design by Jennifer Kelly
Text set in Gotham Rounded Book

The art for this book was made with digital ink,
Dr Pepper, and a good dose of nostalgia

GOODBYE, FRIEND!
HELLO, FRIEND!

Cori Doerrfeld

Dial Books for Young Readers

Every goodbye . . .

. . . leads to a hello.

Goodbye to sitting alone . . .

. . . is hello to sitting together.

Goodbye to outside . . .

. . . is hello to inside.

Goodbye to snowmen . . .

. . . is hello to puddles!

Goodbye to long walks . . .

butterflies . . .

. . . and the sun . . .

. . . is hello to long talks . . .

fireflies . . .

. . . and the stars.

Goodbye to an empty bowl . . .

. . . is hello to a full heart.

Goodbye to only watching . . .

. . . is hello to joining in.

Goodbye to almost giving up . . .

. . . is hello to one more try.

Goodbye to superpowers . . .

. . . is hello to sweet dreams.

But sometimes, when you least expect it, a goodbye comes along that really feels like the end. Sometimes, goodbye is the last thing you want to say.

Like when goodbye to holding tight . . .

. . . is hello to letting go.

But no matter what . . .

goodbye to today . . .

. . . is hello to tomorrow.

Because every goodbye . . .

. . . leads to a hello.